BloodHounds, INC.

1

The Ghost of KRZY

Bill Myers

BETHANY HOUSE PUBLISHERS
MINNEAPOLIS, MINNESOTA 55438

Published by Bethany House Publishers
A Ministry of Bethany Fellowship, Inc.
11300 Hampshire Avenue South
Minneapolis, Minnesota 55438

Printed in the United States of America.

Library of Congress Cataloging-in-Publication Data

Myers, Bill, 1953–
    The ghost of KRZY / by Bill Myers.
       p. cm. — (Bloodhounds, Inc. ; 1)
    Summary: Sean and Misty, a brother and sister detective team, investigate some thefts and mysterious electrical disturbances at their father's radio station.
    ISBN 1–55661–890–5 (pbk.)
    [1. Brothers and sisters—Fiction. 2. Christian life—Fiction. 3. Mystery and detective stories.]
I. Title. II. Series: Myers, Bill, 1953–   Bloodhounds, Inc. ; 1.
PZ7.M98234Gh 1997
[Fic]—dc21   97–21042
                                                        CIP
                                                        AC

To **Tony Wilson** *and* **Dave Meisner,**
committed men of God
who were gracious enough
to let me run with this.
Thanks, guys.

BILL MYERS is a youth worker and a creative writer and film director who co-created the "McGee and Me!" book and video series and whose work has received over forty national and international awards. His many youth books include THE INCREDIBLE WORLDS OF WALLY McDOOGLE, JOURNEYS TO FAYRAH, as well as his teen books, *Hot Topics, Tough Questions* and *Forbidden Doors*. He also writes and acts for Focus on the Family's *Odyssey* radio series.

Contents

There is **no fear** *in love.*
But perfect love drives out **fear.**

1 JOHN 4:18 NIV

1

The Case Begins

TUESDAY, 04:27 PDST

It was happening again. . . .

Up on the hill.

The flickering. An eerie, blue-green light pulsed and glowed through the windows of the deserted radio station.

There was no one inside the building this time of morning. At least no one was supposed to be inside. Mr. Hunter had made sure to lock it up tight when he had finished his final newscast at midnight.

He always did.

Especially with the recent rumors about the place being haunted.

Not that he believed them. As a committed Christian,

he knew there were no such things as ghosts. The Bible makes it clear that once we die, we go to face God. No dropping by seances to say "hi," and no hanging around haunting spooky old radio stations. Once we're gone, we're gone.

But still, there were all those questions. . . .

Like the station being built near an old Indian burial ground. Could that have somehow upset the "spirits"?

And what about the sound? That strange, unearthly noise? In some ways it was almost like—

There it was now. From the building. A voice. High and crackly. Human and yet not human.

Not human at all . . .

The flickering lights and the eerie voice would continue from now until dawn. And then they would disappear.

Until the next time . . .

Yes, sir, ghosts or no ghosts, if there was one place you didn't want to hang around this time of night, it was radio station KRZY.

Because if the place wasn't haunted, it was sure doing a good job of imitating it.

TUESDAY, 07: 00 PDST

"Good morning, Midvale. It's straight up 7:00 A.M. here at KRZY." The voice of Melissa Hunter's dad boomed through her radio alarm clock. She stirred as her father, who was broadcasting from the radio station, continued to speak.

"And if my two kids are out there listening . . . Misty, Sean? You've got until the end of this next song to make it down here to the station for that interview I promised."

Melissa's eyes exploded open.

Interview! That's right. This was the morning! Dad had promised them free air time on his radio station to talk about their new detective agency.

But she'd overslept. So had Sean. And now Dad was giving them only one song to get up, get dressed, and hightail it down to the station.

Impossible!

The station was half a mile away. Maybe he was just kidding. Maybe it was another one of his practical jokes. He was good at those. Or maybe, if they were lucky, he'd do a newscast before the song, then the weather and the stock-market report, and—

11

Suddenly the song began.

So much for luck.

"And, kids," she heard him chuckle over the intro, "don't forget to brush your teeth."

Melissa rolled out of bed. Without her contacts she was pretty much blind, but she'd worry about them later. Besides, as a neat freak, she didn't have to sweat stumbling over anything on her floor. All she had to do was worry about—

BONK!

"Ow!"

Remembering where the wall was.

Once she found the door, she staggered into the hallway and down to Sean's room.

"Sean!" She pounded on his door. "Sean, wake up!"

Nothing but muffled groans on the other side.

More pounding. *"Sean!"*

Repeat in the groans department.

Well, like it or not, there was only one way to wake up her brother. It was a radical approach, one she saved only for emergencies. But this morning was definitely an emergency.

She turned down the hall and called, "Slobs! Come here, girl."

Immediately a giant bloodhound lumbered around the hall from the kitchen. She was black and tan, and stood higher than Melissa's knees. She'd been a gift from her parents . . . a year before Mom had been diagnosed with cancer.

"In here, girl, in here!" Melissa threw open Sean's door. Slobbers slid around the corner, raced into her brother's room, and leaped onto his bed . . . all one hundred and two pounds of her.

"*SLOBS!*" he cried.

Good, he was awake.

Now would come the usual screams and hollers since, as you may have guessed, Slobbers didn't get her name by accident. In fact, at that very moment, she was covering Sean in affectionate slobbers, licks, and drool. *Lots* of drool. It was a bloodhound specialty.

"*MISTY!*"

Yes, sir, her brother would be out of bed in no time.

TUESDAY, 07:00 PDST

Meanwhile, at that exact moment, just a few blocks away, KC, Spalding, and Bear were hiding in the bushes.

Together the three of them crouched on their bikes, watching . . . waiting . . .

"It's already 7:00," KC complained. She was the tomboy of the group. Short but tough. She had a voice so husky it sounded like she ate sandpaper for breakfast, then washed it down with a box of nails. She was also the not-so-proud owner of a new set of braces, which she kept picking and fiddling with. "You sure he's gonna come by here?" she growled.

Spalding, who was as rich and spoiled as KC was tough and mean, checked his Rolex watch and said, "Patience, child. Bear is certain the man uses this route every morning. Isn't that correct, Bear?"

Bear, the third member of the group, was doing what he did best. Sleeping.

"Bear? *Bear!*"

The large, roly-poly boy startled awake. Not exactly being the brains of the group, he answered with a clear and resounding, "Huh?"

"You said he comes by this way nearly every morning," Spalding said.

"Huh?" Bear repeated.

"The hermit? On the bike? Remember why we're here?"

"Oh yeah," Bear yawned, "and we're gonna get him good. Real good."

"That's right," KC agreed. "Who's he think he is, hidin' out in that house all the time? Only comin' out at night. It ain't natural."

"That's right," Spalding said, straightening his tie. "Father says the man's presence in the neighborhood is adversely affecting property value. The sooner he vacates our area the better."

"And we're gonna help him do just that," KC snickered.

"Precisely," Spalding said.

"Zzzz . . ." Bear snored.

Suddenly KC spotted something and pointed. "What's that?"

Both looked up the street. A dark form was coming into view over the hill. The sun rose directly behind it, making it impossible to see all the details. Except it was somebody on a bike . . . wearing a long black overcoat . . . and a hat.

"It's him!" KC shouted.

"Excellent!" Spalding responded.

"Zzzz . . ." Bear replied.

"Bear," KC hissed, "Bear, wake up!"

She gave him a punch in the gut, and he startled awake.

"Here he comes now," Spalding whispered. "Everybody nice and quiet."

The mysterious figure continued his approach.

All hands gripped their handlebars. Feet pressed down on the bike pedals as they waited in anticipation.

"Steady . . ." KC warned, "steady . . ."

The dark figure was nearly there.

"Easy . . ."

Then at last, he passed.

"After him!" KC yelled.

All three kids pushed off. Their bicycles shot out of the bushes as they began the chase.

The stranger threw a look over his shoulder. Between his long coat with the turned-up collar and his hat, it was impossible to see his face. It was always that way. Ever since he'd moved in nearly six months ago, no one had ever seen him close up. No one had even talked to him.

He wouldn't let them.

KC, Spalding, and Bear were about to change all of that. They were going to force him to make contact. They were going to scare the daylights out of him. And they were going to make him sorry he'd ever moved to Middleton.

As you've no doubt guessed, these three were not particularly interested in winning the Mr. Nice Guy (or Guyette) Award. At the moment they had one and only one purpose. . . .

"Get him!" Bear yelled.

The stranger pedaled as fast as he could. Unfortunately, his bike was an old clunker and no match for the kids' multiple-speed bikes. They quickly closed in on him.

He was less than fifty feet ahead. In a matter of seconds, they'd catch up and force him off the road. After that . . . well, who knew? But whatever they did, they'd make sure he understood he was not welcome.

Suddenly the stranger veered off to the left, heading down Sycamore Street.

"Where's he going?" KC shouted. "He don't live down there."

"I'm uncertain!" Spalding yelled. "But he is not going to elude our capture. Not this time. *After him!*"

2

What Was That?

"Come on, Misty!" Sean pounded on the bathroom door. "Let's go, let's go!"

"Just give me another second," Melissa called from inside.

"The song's been playing for over a minute. What's taking you so long?"

But of course Sean didn't need an answer. Having grown up with a sister for the past twelve years, he already knew. *Girls . . .* he sighed, *give 'em a mirror, a brush, and a bathroom, and they'll always be late. It's like a law or something.*

Finally the door opened and Melissa appeared, her hair dripping wet.

"You washed your hair?" Sean asked in unbelief.

"Of course," she answered, scooting past him. "I'm going out in public, aren't I?"

Sean could only stare. His sister was getting weirder by the week.

"Hurry up," she shouted, "or we're going to be late!"

KC, Spalding, and Bear continued closing in on the stranger. He was less than ten feet away.

"Proceed to his left side," Spalding shouted. "Bear and I shall approach him from the right."

"Okay!" KC yelled.

They quickly pulled beside him until he was surrounded. Even at this distance, his face was blocked by his hat and coat collar. But not for long. In just a moment they would ram into him, causing him to crash. In just a moment they'd finally reveal his true identity for all the world to see.

"All right," KC yelled. "Let's get him."

Spalding nodded. He and Bear swerved in toward the stranger from the right. KC swung in from the left. But just before they hit, the stranger reached down to a lever on his handlebars and pulled it. There was a loud *swoosh* and more smoke than when it's your sister's night to cook.

Unbelievably, the stranger had disappeared. He was no longer there. Well, he was there, but instead of between them, he was eight feet *above* them!

The kids were traveling too fast to turn back. They crashed into each other with more than your usual amount of screams and broken body parts.

Meanwhile, the stranger's wheels landed on the sidewalk up ahead with the same squeal a 757's wheels make when they hit the runway. He then zoomed off faster than ever.

Melissa and Slobs were the first to race out of the garage—Slobs on a leash and Misty rattling down the driveway behind him on her in-line skates.

A moment later Sean appeared on his skateboard. He was washing down his fifth minidoughnut with a quart of milk.

"How much time?" he shouted as he passed them.

21

"I'm guessing about a minute and a half!" Melissa yelled.

They bore down harder.

Starting a private detective agency had originally been Sean's idea. As the older of the two (by a whole eleven months), he figured he had the wisdom, the athletic ability, and the incredible good looks (not to mention the giant, econo-sized ego) to pull it off. Melissa, on the other hand, had the brains, neatness, and common sense that her brother obviously lacked. Together they formed a terrific company.

Well, except for the part of not getting any work.

The Bloodhound Detective Agency had been in business two weeks now, and so far no one had offered to hire them.

"We gotta advertise," Sean had insisted. "That's what's missing."

For once, Melissa had to admit her brother was right. That's when they started wearing down Dad. That's when they convinced him to let them talk about their agency on his radio station.

It was a great plan . . . except for the part of having to make it to the station in the next minute and thirty-four seconds.

Make that a minute and thirty-two seconds. . . .

Er, one minute and twenty-nine . . .

Well, you get the idea.

Unfortunately, Sean was in the middle of a long swig of milk and didn't see Mrs. Tubbs, their cranky neighbor from down the street. She was decked out in five thousand pink hair curlers and her favorite flowered bathrobe. She was also busy yelling at the men who were delivering her plush, wall-to-wall white carpeting.

". . . and your hands," she complained, "they better be clean. That's very expensive carpeting you're handling. And my petunias. Watch my petunias!"

The men had just unloaded the carpet from their van and were crossing the sidewalk with the giant roll.

That's when Melissa spotted them.

"Sean, look out!"

Sean lowered his milk carton just in time to see the roll of carpeting dead ahead.

Melissa screamed.

Mrs. Tubbs screamed.

The delivery men screamed.

Unfortunately, everybody was so busy screaming that no one thought of moving the carpet.

In a last-ditch effort, Sean leaped from his

skateboard. The board scooted under the roll of carpet while Sean sailed over the top . . . landing perfectly back on the board on the other side.

"All right!" he shouted, "Sean Hunter does it again!" He threw a look over his shoulder to see how Melissa was faring. She had ducked down and was just shooting under the roll. Sean was impressed . . . even if she was his sister.

But instead of applauding their efforts, Mrs. Tubbs did what she did best. Complain. "You Hunter kids, you're nothing but trouble!"

"I'm sorry, Mrs. Tubbs," Melissa shouted over her shoulder.

But Mrs. Tubbs was definitely in one of her moods. She stomped around, shouting sarcastically, " 'I'm sorry, Mrs. Tubbs. I'm sorry, Mrs. Tubbs.' I'll have you know this carpeting cost me—"

Unfortunately, in the midst of her little tantrum, Mrs. Tubbs had accidentally kicked the automatic sprinkler valve . . . which accidentally turned on all the front yard sprinklers . . . which sent the delivery men racing back and forth, trying to get out of the water.

No problem . . . except for the part where they knocked into Mrs. Tubbs, sending her face first into the flower bed full of . . . you guessed it, her prized petunias.

When she finally rose, the entire front half of her looked like a giant mud ball.

Even that wouldn't have been so bad if it hadn't been for the delivery men. They were so busy laughing that they accidentally dropped the roll of carpet.

No problem . . . except for the part where it fell to the ground and began to quickly unroll . . . directly toward Mrs. Tubbs.

Her eyes widened as it raced toward her. And being the thoughtful, intellectual-type person she was, she did what any thoughtful, intellectual-type person would do. She screamed her head off.

"AUGHHHH!"

KC, Spalding, and Bear had scrambled back onto their bikes. Although they were bruised and their bicycles were more twisted than a piece of modern sculpture, they were not about to give up. Rocket-powered bicycle or no rocket-powered bicycle, they were going to catch the mysterious stranger.

In a matter of seconds, they had caught up to him

and were closing in. But instead of getting too close (they figured one crash n' burn routine a day was enough) they began yelling and screaming, doing all they could to scare the poor guy.

And it worked. He was so shook up that he didn't see Sean and Melissa rounding the corner in front of him.

"WOOAAA . . ."

"WAAHHH . . ."

That was Sean and Melissa screaming (don't ask me which one was which) as they swerved to opposite sides. Fortunately, they missed him. Unfortunately, they didn't miss KC, Spalding, and Bear, who were right behind.

"LOOK OUT!"

"GET OUT OF THE WAY!"

"WE'RE GOING TO—"

All five crashed into one another. I'll save you the gory details. Let's just say on a scale of one to ten, this was definitely pushing an eleven. Bent handlebars here, broken wheels there. And all sorts of knees wrapped around shoulders, heads sticking out of armpits, and legs twisted into cute little pretzels.

But there was still one more catastrophe to go. . . .

Half a block away, Mrs. Tubbs' carpeting continued unrolling toward her. It wasn't until the very last second that she managed to leap onto the sidewalk and barely miss being hit.

That is until the stranger on the bicycle suddenly slammed into her, sending her mud-drenched body flying face first onto the white carpet.

KER-SPLAT.

She groaned slightly and rolled onto her back, leaving a perfect photocopy (or should I say mudcopy) of her front side on the white carpeting.

Meanwhile, down the street, Sean and Melissa were busy untangling themselves from twelve other arms and legs, not to mention a few bikes, skateboards, and in-line skates thrown in to complicate matters.

"Look what you did to my buckle!" Bear complained as he staggered to his feet and examined his giant Texas-shaped belt buckle. "You bent my buckle. You bent my buckle!"

"What were you doing racing around like that in the first place?" Sean demanded.

By now all five kids were on their feet, arguing as they checked for broken bones and misplaced organs.

"We almost had him, too!" little KC complained.

"Almost had who?" Melissa asked.

Spalding, who was busy looking for scratches on his

expensive Rolex watch, answered, "Why, that hermit fellow down the street, of course."

"You mean that sicko who's always sneaking around at night?" Sean asked.

"Sean . . ." Melissa warned.

"What?"

"We don't even know him," she said.

"What's to know?" Sean asked. "The guy's definitely weird."

KC nodded. "Probably a psycho."

"A definite liability to the neighborhood," Spalding added as he took off his glasses and cleaned them.

Then suddenly, amidst all of these voices, a brand-new one was heard.

"You may be right," the voice said in a high, almost electronic sound. "But never judge a book by its silver lining."

All five kids froze.

"What was that?" Bear asked.

"I . . . I don't know," KC answered nervously.

"I believe it came from the vicinity of your coat pocket," Spalding said.

All eyes turned to KC's jean jacket. Slowly, very slowly, she reached inside her pocket. "All I got is this

28

here lighter . . . and my computer game," she said as she pulled them out. "But the game ain't on, and it don't talk or nothin', so it can't—"

Suddenly she gasped.

"What's wrong?" Bear asked. "KC, what's wrong?"

KC tried to answer, but all she could do was make little wheezing sounds as she pointed at the computer game screen.

The others quickly moved around to see for themselves.

There on the screen was a little 3-D cartoon character. He had bright red hair and wore a neon suit that seemed to crackle and short out, changing colors and patterns every other second.

No one said a word, except for Slobs, who sniffed at the game and started to whine.

The cartoon creature looked over to the side of the screen, almost as if he could see the animal. "Good girl," his electric voice cracked nervously. "Good doggie."

The kids continued to stare, speechless.

Turning to them, the little guy gave a quick wave. "Gotta go. See ya later, crocodile."

And then he was gone. Just like that.

Completely vanished.

As if he'd never been there at all. . . .

29

3

The Plot Sickens

TUESDAY, 07:42 PDST

"But, Dad," Sean protested, "to start a detective agency these days, you need all sorts of cool electro gizmos and spy gadgets."

"That's right," Melissa agreed. "And we can't buy gizmos and gadgets without money."

"And we can't get money without work."

"And we can't get work without advertising."

There, they'd said it. Now all they had to do was wait for their father to come out from under the control board where he was working. Then he'd throw open his arms, say he completely understood, and offer them all the free air time to advertise on his station that they wanted.

Either that or they'd have to deal with reality.

"I don't think so, guys," Dad answered from somewhere underneath the board.

(Reality, what a miserable concept.)

"Why not?" Melissa asked.

At last he slid out and glanced up at his kids. He was a good-looking man, as far as dads go. A touch on the overfed side, with a definite mischievous twinkle. Unfortunately, he was also very overworked. Running a radio station and being a single parent can do that to a person.

He glanced at the digital readout over the board. He had a minute and twenty-two seconds left on the CD that was playing before he had to go back on the air. "Listen," he sighed. "I booked you for an interview to talk about the Bloodhound Detective Agency this morning, right?"

"Right."

"At 7:00, right?"

"Right."

"And you never showed."

"But we had a good reason," Melissa argued.

"That's right," Sean said. "It's hard to get up that early when you're sneaking downstairs and playing computer games till 3:00 in the morning."

Dad gave him a look.

So did Melissa—not quite as kindly.

Dad rose to his feet and crossed over to the window. Outside, Herbie, the station's engineer, was working away on his prized motorcycle. It was a beauty, complete with a new sidecar he was currently bolting to it. Dad tapped on the window and motioned for him to come inside.

Herbie nodded and started for the door. But not before tripping over his toolbox, which caused him to stumble into the parking meter, which caused him to dump his hot coffee directly into the sidecar's seat. Herbie was great in the engineering department . . . he just wasn't so hot when it came to coordination.

"Come on, Dad," Sean pleaded. "You've got to give us another interview."

Dad crossed back to the control board. "Son, the station's already in hock up to its eyeballs. I can't just keep passing out free air time."

"But we're your only kids," Melissa said in her sweetest, most innocent voice.

Dad looked at her.

She blinked her sweetest, most innocent blink.

He looked at Sean.

33

He blinked his sweetest, most innocent blink.

Yes, sir, there was more sweetness and innocence in this room than in some old *Barney* rerun.

But Dad was no fool. "Nice try, guys." He grinned as he pulled a couple CDs from a rack and placed them into a player.

"But you're supposed to help us," Sean whined.

"*And* to teach you responsibility," Dad answered.

It was Melissa's turn. Time to pull out the big guns. Time to look up to her father and in her most helpless, pitiful voice use the D word:

"*Daddy . . .*"

He looked at her.

"We really learned our lesson this time. *Really*." She was good. Very good.

"That's right." Sean nodded eagerly. "From now on, no computer games after 2:00 A.M."

Melissa threw her brother her world-famous dagger look and tried again.

"So give us another chance. Please . . . *pretty please . . .*" It was an impressive performance, especially the way she got her voice to tremble a little at the end. But Dad wasn't falling for it.

"Sorry, kids, no sale."

"Why not?" Melissa demanded.

"Yeah," Sean said, sulking. "Mom would."

The phrase caught Dad off guard. He turned back to his son and asked, "What's that?"

Sean looked down at the carpet. He knew he'd gone too far, but there was no turning back now. He continued a little more softly, almost mumbling, "If Mom were still here, she'd let us."

Silence filled the room. It had been four months since their mother died. But for Sean, Melissa, and Dad, it felt more like four years. Mom had been the glue that held them together. Always making jokes, always understanding, always being there for them. If anything ever went wrong, she was the one person who could fix it.

Until the breast cancer.

But try as she might, that was the one thing she just couldn't seem to fix.

The last few weeks of her life had been the worst. Then came the funeral. Now the days had slowly turned to weeks, which slowly turned into months. And still the emptiness continued, still the dull ache remained. More than once, each had secretly hoped to see her barging into the kitchen, arms full of groceries, chattering away in her usual excitement.

But of course she never did.

She never would.

Dad cleared his throat, then quietly answered his son, "That's not fair, Sean."

Still looking down at the carpet, Sean shrugged.

Suddenly there was a loud bang at the door.

Everyone looked up to see Herbie trying to enter the broadcast booth but with little success. He gave it a second try, this time while turning the doorknob. And this time it worked. (Amazing how little things like that can help.)

"What's up, boss?" he asked.

Dad motioned toward the control panel he'd been under. "Another circuit board's disappeared," he said. "This time for the mixer."

"That's the third one this month," Herbie said, scratching his head.

"Someone's stealing your circuit boards?" Melissa asked.

"Not someone," Herbie said, glancing around nervously. "More like some*thing*."

"You mean the ghost?" Sean asked.

Herbie gave an uncomfortable smile and tried to swallow.

Sean had his answer.

"I don't know about ghosts," Dad said as he slipped on his headphones. The song was ending, and he was going back on the air. "But even after Herbie installed that electronic lock outside, parts are still mysteriously missing."

Herbie nodded, glancing nervously around. "And there's been no forced entry. No one's ever come in. No one's ever gone out . . . at least no one *human*."

Melissa gave a little shudder as she exchanged glances with Sean. Her father had said there were no ghosts, but she knew the rumors as well as the next person. And it was those rumors that now made little goose bumps rise up all over her arms.

The music ended. Dad scooted behind the microphone and flipped on a switch. "That was Dr. Dan Druff and the Four Flakes," he said in his best announcer voice, "with their new hit single, 'You Got Me Itchin' for You.' "

Grabbing a typed piece of paper, he began to read:

" 'Friends, if you're in the market for buying a car,

37

why not swing on down to Sly Huckster's for the new and used deal of a lifetime.' "

He looked at the kids, rolled his eyes, and continued. " 'Ol' Sly's got dozens of cars, and he's looking for someone just like you to . . .' "

Now that Dad was on the air, it would be impossible to talk to him, so Melissa and Sean followed Herbie out of the broadcast booth.

Moments later they were in the station's combination office, lunchroom, and work area. As usual, Sean was already at the kitchen counter checking out yesterday's stale doughnuts. "So you really think there's a ghost around here?" he asked.

Herbie shrugged. "How else would you explain it?"

"But Dad says there are no such things as ghosts," Melissa answered.

"Maybe not . . ." Herbie said. "But people keep seeing lights and stuff late at night when no one's here. Some even say they've heard voices."

"Voices?" Melissa swallowed.

"Yup. And like your daddy says, ain't no one can get

in or out of the station except me and him. We're the only ones who know the combination to the outside digital lock. Besides—"

Herbie came to a sudden stop.

"What's wrong?" Sean asked, finishing off a crusty maple bar with a burp.

But Herbie said nothing. He only stared at the hot plate beside the sink.

"Herbie?" Melissa asked.

"That teapot . . ." He pointed to an old metal teapot resting on the hot plate. "It's moved again."

"Moved?" Melissa asked, feeling a slight chill creep across her arms and through her shoulders.

Herbie nodded and Sean started to reach for it.

"No, don't touch it!" Herbie practically shouted.

Sean pulled back and Herbie quickly rose to his feet.

"Why not?" Sean asked.

Herbie barely heard him. He was too busy fumbling in his overalls pocket.

Melissa and Sean traded glances. "Herbie . . ." Melissa probed. "Herbie, what's wrong?"

By now Herbie had pulled out three rabbits' feet and was madly rubbing all of them. Not an easy feat when he was also busy crossing his fingers, his arms, his legs, and anything else that could be crossed.

"Herbie . . ."

"Shhh . . ."

They watched as, ever so gently, he snuck up toward the teapot.

"Herbie," Melissa whispered, "what are you doing?"

He arrived at the hot plate and slowly reached toward the pot. Then suddenly remembering, he stopped, closed his eyes, and clicked his heels three times.

Melissa and Sean continued to stare. They'd always known Herbie was a little superstitious, but this was ridiculous.

Ever so carefully, Herbie reached out to the teapot with one hand, grabbed a nearby mug with the other, and began to pour. But instead of tea, it was money that poured out. Dozens of old silver dollars.

"Wow!" Sean cried.

"How'd you do that?" Melissa asked.

"It's not me," Herbie whispered, giving the pot one last shake. "It's this teapot. It moved again last night. And if I rub these here rabbits' feet and do everything just right, sometimes when it's moved, it pours out money instead of coffee."

"That's incredible," Sean exclaimed as he moved to the pot to look it over.

"Sean," Melissa warned, "be careful."

But of course Sean wouldn't listen. After all, he was the big brother and not listening was part of his job. He picked up the pot and looked inside. "You think . . . it might be connected to the ghost?"

Herbie shrugged. "I don't know any other explanation."

"Come on, guys." Melissa swallowed nervously. "There are no such things as ghosts. Remember?"

"I got it!" Sean suddenly exclaimed.

Herbie and Melissa exchanged looks as he set down the teapot and began to pace. "We need more time on the radio to advertise the Bloodhound Detective Agency, right?"

"Right," Melissa said.

"And Dad keeps losing equipment, right?"

"Right."

"So there you have it." Sean beamed.

"All right, way to go, Sean!" Herbie cried.

"Excuse me," Melissa asked. "Did I miss something?"

Herbie looked deflated and turned to Sean. "Did we?"

"A trade-off," Sean answered impatiently. "We stake

out the station, crack the case of the ghost and the missing equipment, and Dad gives us free advertising time."

"Or he puts it toward some serious carpet cleaning," Dad said as he opened the door to the broadcast booth.

Sean and Melissa turned to him. "Huh?"

"Mrs. Tubbs just called. Seems she had a bit of a problem with her new carpeting this morning."

Sean and Melissa looked at each other. Then they sighed in perfect unison. It looked like they had another reason to be earning some money.

Just the same, Melissa wasn't too thrilled about Sean's plan. I mean it was one thing to track down thieves and bad guys.

It was quite another to try to catch a ghost. . . .

4

Getting Ready

TUESDAY, 22:05 PDST

Melissa started down the stairs with a giant armload of suitcases and overnight bags. "This stakeout idea of yours is really lame," she called down to her brother.

Sean stood at the bottom of the stairs, looking up at her through the viewfinder of a still camera. "To solve a crime, we have to be at the scene of the crime."

"What crime?" Melissa argued as she continued down the steps. "Nobody's even broken into the station."

"That stuff didn't just get up and walk out on its own," he pointed out.

"That's right. Maybe it had a little help. . . ." Melissa lowered her voice. "A little *supernatural* help."

"Don't start in with that ghost stuff again."

"Well . . ."

"You're just scared 'cause you don't know what's really going on."

"And you do?" she huffed.

"Of course not." He replaced the lens cap to his camera. "But at least I don't buy into all of this *ghost* business."

Melissa arrived at the foot of the stairs and dumped her stuff onto the growing pile. Of course her brother was right. If she really knew what was going on, she probably wouldn't be as scared. But she didn't, so she was. So there.

"Hey." Sean motioned toward the growing stacks of suitcases. "What is all this stuff? We're only staying overnight."

Melissa shrugged. "Just your basic curling iron, hair dryer, hair spray, makeup, polish, polish remover, and—"

"What's this?" Sean had spotted a small picture frame jutting up from one of her bags. He pulled it out. It was a picture of all four of them . . . including Mom, just before she'd gotten sick. They were on a camping trip, getting rained out, soaked to the skin, and yucking it up.

"You miss her?" Melissa asked quietly.

He nodded. Then looking up at her, he asked, "You?"

Melissa also nodded. "Sometimes at night . . . sometimes my chest hurts so much I can hardly breathe."

Sean looked away. She could tell he was fighting back the emotion. "We better get going" was all he said as he motioned toward the door. "Dad and Slobs are waiting in the van."

TUESDAY, 22:11 PDST

Minutes later they were outside the minivan trying to squeeze all of Melissa's stuff into the back.

The plan for the evening was simple. The two of them would spend the entire night inside the station, taking shifts at staying awake. Then if there was any activity, whoever was up would wake the other and they'd check it out together.

At first Dad had disapproved. But when they had convinced Herbie to stay with them (up in the storage room, where he could sleep on the old sofa), Dad reluctantly agreed.

"You know," Sean said as he continued loading Melissa's pile of junk in the back, "with the right electrical stuff, we wouldn't have to do any of this."

"What do you mean?" she asked, handing him more bags.

"I mean we'd just set up the hidden cameras, turn on the video recorders, and bingo, case solved."

"That's right," Dad teased from the front. "And before you know it, the Bloodhound Detective Agency would become the greatest agency in the city."

"You mean the state," Melissa corrected.

"Guys, guys, guys," Sean interrupted. "It's the nation or nothin'."

"Hey, Hunter!"

Sean and Melissa turned from their packing to see KC, Spalding, and Bear approach on their bikes.

"Hey," Sean called back.

"Tomorrow morning's the big day," Spalding said as they pulled up beside them.

"Big day?" Melissa asked.

"That's right." KC nodded. "We're drivin' that old hermit out of the neighborhood for good."

"You joining us?" Spalding asked.

"Wish I could," Sean answered as he shut the back of the van and crossed around to the passenger side. "But we have this big case to crack."

"Too bad," KC said. "Should be good."

"That's right," Spalding added. "It's going to be *au revoir* to that loser in a big way."

"Yeah," KC said as she pushed off on her bike and started down the street. "Whatever he said, in a *big* way."

Spalding and Bear followed after her.

Sean opened his door and shouted over the roof, "Just make sure you give ol' Jerk Face a little something for me, too."

"Sean," Dad's voice came sternly from the front.

"What?" Sean asked as he and Melissa climbed in.

"You don't talk that way about people."

"It's just that hermit guy the next block over. He's a real creep."

"I don't care who it is," Dad said as he dropped the car into gear and they started off. "You don't talk about anyone like that."

"But the guy's majorly weird," Sean protested.

Dad glanced at him. "And because somebody's weird, that gives you the right to be mean?"

"I'm sure glad that's not how God thinks," Melissa quipped.

"What?" Sean asked.

"If God loved only normal people, then you, big

brother, wouldn't stand a chance."

"Ho-ho, very funny," Sean said. "You guys don't even know that hermit."

Dad glanced over at Sean. "Do you?"

Sean began to answer, then stopped. He hated it when his dad was right.

TUESDAY, 22:16 PDST

Herbie didn't mean to go to sleep. He had every intention of staying awake and greeting the Hunter kids when they arrived with their dad at the station. But he'd been working most of the evening on his motorcycle sidecar, and he was pretty beat.

Besides, their dad knew the combination to the outside door. . . .

And it was so peaceful up in the storage room. . . .

And the old sofa Herbie was stretched out on was so comfortable. . . .

And warm . . .

And cozy . . .

And . . .

Before he knew it, Herbie was taking a stroll through dreamland. Which was too bad, because what was happening downstairs in the broadcast booth and the lunchroom was a lot more interesting than anything he could dream up.

For starters, the computer came on . . . all by itself. No one touched it. No one hit the power switch. But suddenly, down in the broadcast booth, the little green light flickered and the hard disc drive began to whir.

But that was only the beginning. . . .

Next the portable TV in the lunchroom turned on. And then, all by itself, it began to change channels. Very slowly. One channel after another. First the news report, then a black-and-white movie, then some cop show. And it kept turning and turning and turning. . . .

Upstairs, Herbie dreamed about a dirt-bike race he was winning. He was racing his little motorcycle and sidecar against the toughest bikers in the country. The fact that he wore jet black, all-leather coveralls, along with a flowing silk scarf, added a nice touch. But the best part was the passenger in his sidecar. It was the future Mrs. Herbie . . . who coincidentally enough looked exactly like some beautiful supermodel. (What Herbie lacked in coordination, he definitely made up for in imagination.)

Down in the lunchroom, the TV passed a particularly

loud channel, and Herbie stirred slightly . . . until the mute button was hit.

Now there was only silence.

And still the channels changed . . . one after another, until at last they stopped. There was no station on this channel. Nothing but static. But deep inside the static, a form began to appear. A strange, humanlike form that grew larger and larger.

Meanwhile, the Hunter van started up the hill toward the station. It was less than five hundred yards away. If anyone in the van had looked up to the station, they would have seen the blue-green flickering through the windows. They would have seen the light and shadows shifting and changing shape as the creature inside the TV moved across the screen.

But they didn't.

Instead, the unsuspecting passengers drew closer and closer, having no idea of the danger that lay ahead. Back upstairs, Herbie smiled and turned on the sofa. He was now in the winner's circle, being congratulated by Stallone, Schwarzenegger, and all the other cool superhero types he'd just beaten.

From inside the lunchroom, it was possible to hear the crunching gravel as the van approached. And suddenly, just like that, the TV shut down. The picture went off, and there was only the faint crackle as the circuits inside the set began to cool.

The computer did likewise. With any luck, the unsuspecting passengers would not notice that either had been on. But even if they did, it wouldn't matter. Because the creature controlling the TV and the computer would still have its way with them.

It was all part of the plan.

It was all part of the trap.

Regardless of what they said or did, the creature would have its way. . . .

5

The Stakeout

TUESDAY, 22:18 PDST

"So what do you think it is?" Melissa asked her father from the backseat of the van. "I mean if it's not a ghost."

"That's a good question, Misty," Dad said as they continued up the hill toward the station. "The best Herbie and I can figure is it's some sort of electromagnetic disturbance."

"But that wouldn't describe the missing electronic parts," Sean insisted.

"Or the teapot with all the money," Melissa added.

Dad pursed his lips and blew softly. "You're right. But no one has been leaving or entering the station, I can tell you that. Otherwise I wouldn't let you stay. No one knows the code to that outside lock but Herbie and me."

"At least no one mortal," Melissa said.

"Would you knock it off with the ghost stuff," Sean protested. Even though he didn't believe in the ghost theory, it was obvious she was giving him the willies.

"Just because we don't understand something doesn't mean that it's supernatural," Dad explained, "or that it's even bad."

"That's exactly what I've been telling her," Sean agreed. "She's just afraid because she doesn't know. As soon as we find out what's really going on at the station, it won't be scary like that at all."

"That's right." Melissa swallowed hard. "It might be worse."

Dad threw her a look in the rearview mirror. "Are you really frightened about staying, Misty?"

She shrugged. "A little."

"Because if you are, you two don't have to stay here toni—"

"No, she's not afraid," Sean suddenly interrupted. "At least not that much." He turned to give her a stern look. "Are you, Misty? You're not *that* afraid."

Melissa returned her brother's look. She knew that if she admitted her fear, she could jeopardize the entire mission. If she said she was afraid, Dad would turn around and head right back home. But if she said she wasn't afraid and they actually stayed, then there was a chance she'd wind up as some ghost's late-night snack.

Decisions, decisions . . .

She glanced back at Sean. It was clear the stakeout was important to him. It was also clear that the fate of the entire Bloodhound Detective Agency rested on her decision. So with quiet determination, she cranked up a little smile and croaked, "I'll be okay."

She heard Sean let out a sigh of relief and saw Dad glance at him.

"You know," Dad cleared his throat. "Fear of the unknown is a funny thing. It doesn't just start and stop with so-called ghosts."

"What do you mean?" Sean asked.

"I mean it has to do with people, too."

"People?"

Dad looked at him. "Like hermits or 'majorly weird' people who live down the block that we don't fully understand."

"What are you—" Suddenly Sean's eyes narrowed. "Oh, you mean like that nutcase KC and the guys are going after tomorrow morning."

"Exactly," Dad said. "The three of them are tormenting him and calling him names for the very same reason Misty's afraid. They simply don't understand him, they simply don't know."

"That's right," Misty chimed in, grateful to be off the hook. "If you knew him, I bet you'd really like him."

"Yeah, like a bad case of the flu."

"No, seriously," Dad said. "Fear, hatred, prejudice . . . they all come from the same thing. Ignorance. The Bible says perfect love casts out all fear. If you two really knew how loved you are by God, then you'd trust that He'd watch over and protect you wherever you are . . . even at the station."

"Hear that?" Sean called back to Misty.

"*And,*" Dad continued, "if you really knew this hermit guy and set out to show him love, you wouldn't be afraid of him, either."

Sean fidgeted. It was one thing to straighten Misty out on life's truths, but quite another to be picked on himself.

Suddenly from the backseat Slobs let out a booming bark. Everyone jumped as she lumbered to her feet and continued.

"What is it, girl?" Melissa asked. "What's wrong?"

Sean peered through the windshield. The station was just ahead. But he could see nothing unusual.

And still Slobs kept barking.

"Easy, girl, easy . . ."

"What's her problem?" Sean complained.

"I don't know," Dad said as he pulled the van up to the front steps of the station. "But she's definitely seeing or hearing—"

And then he stopped.

"What on earth . . ."

Sean turned to him. "What's wrong?"

His father was staring at the digital clock on the dashboard.

"Dad?" Sean asked, his nervousness growing. "Dad!"

At last Dad shook his head. "That was the weirdest thing. That clock there."

"Yeah?"

"For a second all of the numbers were dancing around, coming together and forming a . . . a . . ."

"A what?" Melissa asked anxiously. "Dad, what did you see?"

"Nothing . . . but for a brief second, they almost looked like they'd formed a little man . . . a cartoon character."

57

Sean and Melissa exchanged looks.

"Well, it's gone now," Dad said as he turned off the van and opened the door. "Probably just a short in the clock . . . or in my imagination." He gave them a grin. "Let's get your stuff unpacked and set up your stakeout."

"Yeah," Sean said, glancing at the station a little more nervously.

"Yeah," Melissa said, glancing at the station *a lot* more nervously.

TUESDAY, 22:16 PDST

Minutes later everything was sprawled out in the broadcast booth of the station—sleeping bags unrolled, pillows pulled out, and overnight necessities scattered everywhere.

In Melissa's case these necessities included a small vanity mirror, toothbrush, toothpaste, dental floss, hair curlers, hair spray, moisturizing cream, shampoo, conditioner, slippers, pajamas, and robe. Then of course there were the several changes of clothes in case she couldn't make up her mind what to wear tomorrow.

Girls . . . sheesh.

Sean's overnight supplies were slightly less . . . just the

clothes on his back, which he planned to sleep in and which he'd also been wearing for the past four days.

Boys . . . sheesh.

Even though they were unpacked and ready to start the stakeout, Dad kept finding excuses to hang around. If he wasn't checking on equipment, he was rearranging CDs or straightening papers or dusting shelves or stacking and restacking the tissues inside the tissue box or—

"Dad," Sean said.

He turned to his son. "Hmm?"

Sean just looked at him.

Obviously caught, Dad gave an embarrassed grin. "Oh, right." He cleared his throat nervously. "I, uh . . ."

"It's okay," Melissa said sympathetically. "Don't worry about us. We'll be fine."

"Yeah," Sean said with a mischievous twinkle. "What was it you were saying about perfect love casting out all fear?"

"Besides, Herbie's upstairs," Melissa added.

"And we have Slobs," Sean said, "so there's absolutely nothing for you to worry about."

Dad nodded and fidgeted.

"So you'll be going now, right?" Sean asked.

"Hmm?"

"Home?" Sean repeated, motioning toward the door, carefully explaining, "Door . . . car . . . home . . . you?"

"Oh, right. I guess . . . uh, I'll be heading home now."

"Hey, that's a great idea," Sean teased.

Dad nodded and started for the door. "Well, um . . ." He fumbled with the door handle. "You kids sleep tight, and I'll see you first thing in the morning."

"Bye," they repeated for what felt like the billionth time.

"Uh, right. Bye-bye." At last he headed into the office and out the front door—but not before making sure it was locked about a hundred times before finally leaving.

Dads . . . sheesh.

"Okay," Sean said as he crossed the room, rubbing his hands together and forming a plan. "I'll take the first shift and—"

"No way," Melissa interrupted. "You'd let me sleep through all of the action."

Sean gave her a look. Sometimes sisters could be more of a pain than dads. "Okay then, you take the first shift and I'll—"

"Right, and if something happens on the second shift instead?"

"Okay, fine," Sean snapped. "Then we'll both stay awake."

"That's fine with me," Melissa shot back.

"Okay, fine!" Sean said as he slumped into the nearest chair.

"Fine!" Melissa sighed as she folded her arms and sat on the counter.

Together they stayed in the room, arms crossed, doing their best to out-stubborn each other. But the truth of the matter was they were both glad the other was awake to keep them company. There was also another truth. It had to do with the lateness of the night and the fact that after a while they were both bored out of their minds.

Neither had brought games or books to keep them occupied. And before they knew it, they had both decided to crawl into their sleeping bags . . .

. . . just to stay warm.

Then to stretch out . . .

. . . just to get comfortable.

Then to close their eyes . . .

. . . just to give them a little rest.

Until finally, both of them had dropped off to sleep. Sean and Melissa in their sleeping bags, Slobs sprawled out between them, snoring away.

They would remain like that until it was nearly dawn.

WEDNESDAY, 05:49 PDST

Once again the portable TV in the lunchroom clicked on by itself, and once again it began to glow. It was the no-station channel with all the static. But the mute button was on, so it was perfectly silent. Soon the eerie figure appeared. It came forward and began peering around the edges of the screen.

It saw nothing.

A moment later the computer in the broadcast booth also came on. Its hard disc whirred and the monitor glowed. The figure from the TV was now on this screen. Carefully, it peeked around the edges, surveying the room until it spotted the two children and the dog sleeping on the floor.

Meanwhile, the electronic lock on the front door began to click and ping as the four secret numbers to the combination were activated.

The door was now unlocked.

Ever so slowly, it opened. A dark, shadowy form silently entered the office and drifted across the room.

But instead of going into the broadcast booth, it glided back to the lunch area.

It arrived at the hot plate and reached out to the teapot. Carefully, one gloved hand picked it up while the other produced a handful of rare silver dollars. Then one at a time, ever so silently, it dropped the money into the pot.

When it was finished, it replaced the teapot on the hot plate.

Now it was time to begin its work. A work that, if Sean, Melissa, and Slobs were lucky, they would continue to sleep through and never know about.

Unfortunately, there was another force in that radio station. A force that had been passing through the walls and roaming the rooms. A force that would see to it they would not sleep. A force that would launch them into an adventure they would never have been able to imagine—not even in their wildest dreams.

6

It's Show Time, Folks

WEDNESDAY, 06:35 PDST

Melissa was the first to stir from sleep. Against her closed eyelids she saw movement. Little flickerings of light. With great determination and her world-famous strong will, she finally pried them open.

When she did, she wished she hadn't.

Because there on the desk right above their heads, the computer monitor was glowing all by itself. Normally, that would have been enough to surprise anybody. But there was one other little shocker. . . .

A tiny character stood inside the screen. The same one with the frizzy red hair and shorting-out clothing they had seen on KC's computer game.

"Psst . . ." he motioned to her. "Psssst."

Melissa glanced around. No way could he be talking to her. After all, he was just a character on a screen.

"Excuse me . . ." the little guy called. "Excuse me?"

Melissa looked back at the screen. It was the weirdest sensation, having an image on a computer screen act like it could actually see you. Of course she knew that was impossible.

But still . . .

Keeping a wary eye on the monitor, she reached over and gave Sean a poke.

He grumbled and turned his back to her.

"It's getting late," the character on the screen said in a crackly little voice. "And a stitch in time always catches the worm."

Melissa frowned. She reached over and gave Sean another poke. Harder.

He groaned. Louder.

"Sean . . ." she whispered, "Sean, wake up."

"Wha . . . what is it?" he mumbled.

"Wake up."

At last he opened his eyes.

"Hi there," the character on the screen said.

Sean turned and stared.

The character gave a wave. "Good morning."

Suddenly Sean was wide awake and sitting straight up.

"I don't want to be a brother," the character said, "but it's time to get this snow on the road."

Melissa and Sean turned to each other. But before they could respond, there was a noise from the next room. All three—Melissa, Sean, and the computer character—turned their heads to listen. It was so loud that even good ol' Slobs, the ever faithful watchdog, almost woke up.

Almost.

Melissa turned back to the screen. The creature gave a little shrug, then a wave, and suddenly, *poof,* just like that, he was gone.

She turned to her brother, who was staring at the screen with equal astonishment.

"What . . . what was that?" he asked.

Melissa tried to speak, but no words would come out. There was more noise.

"Somebody's in the next room," Sean croaked.

"No kidding," Melissa whispered.

"We better investigate."

"What do you mean, 'we'?" Melissa whispered. "You're the oldest."

"What's that got to do with anything?"

Melissa shrugged. "It doesn't, but I thought I'd give it a try."

"Come on." Silently, he rose to his feet and started toward the door.

Melissa hesitated.

"Misty."

Reluctantly, she rose and followed. "All right, all right," she whispered. "But if we die, you're gonna to live to regret it."

Sean arrived at the door and silently pushed it open.

Melissa followed right behind.

Sean turned and whispered over his shoulder, "Slobs . . . come here, girl. Come on."

And being the great watchdog she was, Slobs turned, groaned, and went back to sleep.

Sean sighed and started through the door. Melissa followed. They entered the office and quietly shut the door behind them. It took a moment for their eyes to adjust to the light. Then they saw him. . . .

The intruder.

He was over at Herbie's workbench, carefully stuffing another piece of electronic equipment into his dark overcoat. Melissa was the first to recognize him. "It's the hermit!" she whispered.

Sean motioned for her to be quiet. They dropped behind the reception desk, out of sight.

"So I was too hard on him?" Sean whispered, quoting the lecture he'd received last night. "I was judging him 'cause I didn't know him. Well, what do you say now?" he demanded.

Melissa looked at him. What could she say? Apparently the hermit down the street, the one KC, Spalding, and Bear were tormenting, wasn't only weird . . . he was also a thief. The very thief who had been stealing and robbing from the station!

Sean moved in for a better look, but the stranger was no longer in sight. Silently, Sean rose to his feet.

"Be careful," Melissa whispered.

"Relax, I know what I'm doing." With that bit of overconfidence, he stealthily raised his foot to step over her. Unfortunately, he set it down directly inside a wastepaper basket.

No problem . . . except for the part where he couldn't get it off . . . which caused him to lose his balance and begin clanking and clunking across the floor . . . which caused him to stumble . . . which caused him to fall on

69

his face directly at the feet of the stranger.

Melissa screamed in terror. Sean would have joined in, but it's hard to scream when you're paralyzed with fear.

Meanwhile, still upstairs dreaming of the winner's circle, Herbie was enjoying Clint Eastwood's pleas to come to Hollywood to give him tough-guy lessons. That is until Sean's bangs and Melissa's screams woke him with a start, causing him to leap from the sofa.

Not a bad move, except for the part where he leaped the wrong way and smacked headfirst into a very hard wall. Once again Herbie dropped back onto the sofa. But instead of seeing Clint or Sly or Arnie, he was seeing an entirely different set of stars.

Downstairs, Sean scrambled to his feet and clanked across the room with his wastebasket shoe until he reached the light switch. He snapped it on and flooded the room with blazing light.

Realizing he was trapped, the stranger looked all directions, then suddenly bolted toward Melissa.

Being the professional-type detective she was, Melissa did what any professional-type detective would do. She closed her eyes and screamed her head off.

Upstairs, the scream helped wake Herbie from his

unconsciousness. It was a little harder getting up this time. The stars were still spinning around his head, and the room was still spinning under his feet. But at last he managed to stagger off of the sofa and do his best imitation of coming to their rescue.

"Hang on," he shouted. "I'm coming! I'm coming!"

His progress would have been a little faster if he hadn't taken all the extra time crashing into more walls. But at last he found the stairway. That was the good news. The bad news was he missed the first step and immediately began tumbling and rolling down them.

Meanwhile, shut inside the broadcast booth, Slobs had finally awakened and began barking away. She wasn't sure what she was barking away at, but she figured that was her job, so she better get to it.

As it turned out, the stranger was not going for Melissa. He was heading past her and toward the door. Once there, he pointed a small black box at the digital lock. There were four electronic beeps, and the pins that had locked the door immediately unbolted. With that, he threw open the door and raced into the dark.

"After him!" Sean shouted. "Don't let him get away."

But letting him get away was exactly what Melissa had in mind. She was grateful that he hadn't tried to hurt her, and she felt no particular need to race outside to see if he had second thoughts on the matter.

Not Sean. He was courageous, fearless, and at least in Melissa's mind, incredibly stupid. With the wastebasket still on his foot, he tromped toward the door in pursuit.

Unfortunately, this was the same time that Herbie finally made it back to his feet at the bottom of the steps and threw open the stairway door. No problem . . . except for the part where it opened smack dab into Sean's face.

Now Sean was the one seeing stars.

After doing a little more stumbling (just for old time's sake) and a little shaking of his head, Sean was finally able to get his bearings and spot the stranger through the door.

"Come on!" he shouted. "He's getting away."

"Who's getting away?" Herbie shouted.

"The thief. Come on!"

Sean clunked past Melissa and out the door. Herbie followed. Reluctantly, Melissa rose to her feet and did likewise. But not before letting Slobs out of the broadcast booth.

Once outside, they caught a glimpse of the stranger.

He was on a bicycle pedaling down the hill as fast as he could.

"He's getting away!" Sean repeated.

"My motorcycle!" Herbie shouted. "You guys hop in the sidecar and I'll drive!"

Sean and Melissa raced to the motorcycle and climbed in. It was a little crowded with Sean's wastebasket foot, but they managed. Until they looked up and saw Slobs, who, not wanting to be left out, came bounding toward them.

"No, Slobs!" Sean shouted. "Down girl, down girl. No!"

But of course she didn't listen and leaped into the air, bringing all one hundred and two pounds of her bloodhound body down on top of them.

"OOOFF!" brother and sister cried in perfect unison. To which Slobs showed her appreciation with plenty of squirming and lots of drooling kisses all over their faces.

Meanwhile, Herbie had hopped onto the motorbike and stomped down on the kick start to fire it up.

Unfortunately, there wasn't a whole lot of fire to fire up. To be more specific, there was none. To be even more specific, the thing wouldn't start.

Herbie tried again, jumping on the kick starter with all of his might.

Ditto in the no-fire department.

And again.

Ditto on the ditto.

"Hurry up!" Sean shouted. "He's getting away!"

"All right, all right. Just give me a second." Herbie hopped off the bike to have a look.

Melissa peered down the road. Dawn was just breaking, and the stranger and his bicycle were silhouetted against the horizon of the blue and pink sky.

Herbie stooped down to the engine and examined it. "It's just these wires," he shouted. "Sometimes they get a little loose."

Carefully, he connected them and—*varoom*, the motorcycle came to life.

That was the good news.

The bad news was the motorcycle was still in gear.

The worse news was that the engine was racing wildly.

And worse than that worse was that the whole contraption took off without Herbie on it.

"Augh!" Melissa shouted as they headed down the road.

"AUGHHH!" Sean shouted, not wanting to be outdone in the yelling department.

"What's going on?" Melissa cried back to Herbie, who was running behind them, trying to catch up. "What's happening?"

"The throttle's stuck!" Herbie yelled.

"What?"

"I said the throttle's stuck. Reach over and unstick the—"

Unfortunately, that was as much as Herbie got out. Because as we've already pointed out, ol' Herb can be a bit on the coordination-challenged side. And before he knew it, his not-so-nimble feet found a not-so-tiny pothole that threw his not-so-little body crashing onto the road.

"HERBIE!" Sean and Melissa shouted.

Herbie was dying to answer, but first he had to check to see if he was alive.

"What do we do?" Sean yelled. "What do we do?"

By the time Herbie made it back to his feet, Sean and Melissa were already out of shouting distance. It was a scary picture, seeing the bosses' kids and their dog crammed into the sidecar of his motorcycle with no one behind the handlebars to drive.

But it was even scarier being the ones crammed into that sidecar.

"Augh . . ." Melissa cried.

"AUUGHHH . . ." Sean cried, still not wanting to be outdone.

"What do we do?" Melissa shouted. "What do we do? What do we do?"

Sean spun around to face the front. Up ahead was the main road. The very same road that ran directly into town. The very same road that would soon be clogged with rush-hour traffic. The very same road they were about to travel down at a gazillion miles an hour with no driver.

Sean looked at Melissa. Melissa looked at Sean. Then they both looked straight ahead and did what they did best.

"AUUGHHHHHHH . . ."

7

The Chase Is On

Now, Sean was no nuclear scientist, but it took only a moment for him to come to this staggering conclusion: If they were about to become major road kill because nobody was steering the motorcycle, maybe it would be a good idea for somebody to try to steer the motorcycle.

Brilliant, huh? (Hey, I told you he was no nuclear scientist.)

Next he began a complex process of elimination, trying to figure out who that somebody should be. The way he saw it, there were three choices:

A. Slobs . . . but she probably didn't have her driver's license. Yet.

B. Melissa . . . but she was just a girl, and his sister at that.

C. Himself . . . always brave, humble, strong, and (did I mention humble?) ready to save the day.

It was a tough decision, but since there was only one real superhero in the group, there was only one choice. . . .

C.

With that in mind, Sean reached down to his foot and pried off the wastebasket—not an easy job with a sister squished beside you and a one-hundred-and-two-pound bloodhound sitting on your lap.

Next he stood in the sidecar and reached over and across to the motorcycle. The best he figured, they were doing about thirty-five miles per hour. Not real fast, but fast enough when you're stretched out between a sidecar and a motorcycle with your face about two and a half feet from the rushing pavement.

"Be careful," Melissa warned.

Sean nodded as he continued to stretch out toward the cycle. He found a large bolt and used it to brace his foot against. A good idea, except that this was the very bolt that held the motorcycle and sidecar together. The

very bolt that he was loosening with each push of his
foot.

And if that wasn't bad enough, there was one other
minor problem. . . .

"Sean . . ." Melissa called.

"Not now!" he shouted.

"Uh, Sean . . ."

"I said not—"

"I think there's something you should see."

"What?" he turned to her angrily.

"That 1984 Buick."

"What 1984 Buick?"

"THE ONE HEADING STRAIGHT FOR US!"

Sean looked up. His eyes widened in terror as he saw
the car coming right at them. In desperation, he gave one
last push against the bolt and made it onto the
motorcycle seat. He quickly grabbed the handlebars and
turned hard to the right.

The car roared by, honking its horn.

"Sorry!" Sean shouted over his shoulder.

"LOOK OUT!" Melissa screamed.

He turned back to see they were racing through a
busy intersection. No problem . . . except for the red light
they'd just gone through.

More honking horns, along with plenty of squealing brakes and shouting people. How they made it through the intersection without becoming someone's hood ornament was anybody's guess. Unfortunately, the loud series of crashes that followed behind them made it clear that the other vehicles weren't quite so lucky.

"Sorry!" Melissa and Sean shouted back in unison.

Neither saw the bolt that Sean had pushed against continue to loosen.

Then Melissa spotted something. "Up ahead. There he is!"

Sean saw him, too. The stranger was just in front of them on his bike. He made a tight left turn, and Sean followed, leaving a fair amount of smoke and rubber on the pavement.

Unfortunately, the force of the turn loosened the bolt even more.

But Sean didn't see it. Rounding that last corner had suddenly added a few other things on his mind . . . like the huge semi blowing its horn and bearing down on them!

"SEAN!"

"I see it, I see it!"

There was no place to go. The semi was directly in

front of them and closing in fast. Instinctively, Sean leaned to the left. Unfortunately, Melissa also had instincts. She leaned to the right.

That was it for the bolt. It finally gave way.

Melissa and Slobs' sidecar broke off and veered to the right. Sean and his motorcycle veered to the left . . . as the semi roared between them, missing both by inches.

It was a close call, but everyone was safe. Well, except for the throttle on Sean's motorcycle still being stuck. . . .

And Melissa's sidecar rolling down the street completely out of control. . . .

Other than that, they were perfectly fine.

WEDNESDAY, 06:51 PDST

Just a few blocks away, KC, Spalding, and Bear hid out at their usual ambush location doing what they did best . . . KC nervously tapping her braces, Spalding checking his Rolex watch, and Bear sleeping. Once again they were ready to attack the mysterious stranger. Only this time it would be a little different. This time they planned to drive him out of the neighborhood for good.

Moments later the stranger raced past them.

"There he is!" Spalding shouted. "After him!"

All three pushed off and began pursuit.

WEDNESDAY, 06:52 PDST

Meanwhile, back at the runaway sidecar, Melissa hung on for dear life as it hit a curb and bounced up onto the sidewalk. For a moment she and Slobs were clear. Well, except for the two mothers who were taking their babies for a stroll.

"Look out!" Melissa shouted, waving her arms. "I can't steer this. I can't steer this!"

As best she could tell, the two mothers understood. At least they seemed to by the way they leaped off the sidewalk with their baby carriages as Melissa raced past.

A moment later Sean was pulling his motorcycle beside her. He was still on the street; she was still on the sidewalk.

"Hang on!" he shouted.

"Well, all right," she yelled. "If you say so!"

Exactly three-quarters of a block away, Mrs. Tubbs was opening her back French doors to a beautiful summer morning. She loved the beautiful songs of the beautiful morning birds . . . the beautiful smell of the beautiful morning air . . . and the beautiful look of her beautiful new carpeting.

Off in the distance, she could hear the irritating roar of an approaching motorcycle. But it made no difference. It was a beautiful morning, and with her beautiful new carpeting, life was simply—you guessed it—*beautiful*.

Meanwhile, Sean pulled closer to Melissa's sidecar.

"Lean over and grab the motorcycle!" he shouted.

Melissa nodded and stretched toward Sean and the cycle. But he was still too far away. "You gotta get closer!" she yelled.

Sean nodded and inched the bike as close to the curb as possible.

Again Melissa tried. This time, for the briefest second, she caught the edge of the seat . . . until the sidecar drifted away.

"Again!" Sean shouted. "Stretch as far as you can!"

Melissa obeyed, stretching and straining for all she was worth. At last the tips of her fingers again grabbed hold of the seat.

"All right!" Sean shouted. "Now hang on! Just hang on!"

Melissa nodded. Things were finally looking up. Well, except for the part about the fire hydrant. When she looked ahead, it was coming straight for them at a zillion and a half miles per hour.

If she continued hanging on to the cycle, they'd hit it.

If she let go, she'd again roll out of control.

Decisions, decisions. To die or not to die, that is the question.

Fortunately, Sean helped make up her mind by shouting, "Let go, or you'll get us killed!"

Melissa saw his point. Not only did she let go, she gave a little push just to make sure.

The good news was they missed the fire hydrant.

The bad news was she didn't miss the fence. The very fence that surrounded the side of Mrs. Tubbs' backyard.

Well, it had surrounded Mrs. Tubbs' backyard. Now part of it was completely flattened by Melissa's sidecar. But that was only the beginning. Next the sidecar raced across her yard, through her freshly watered vegetable garden, and directly toward poor Mrs. Tubbs, who stood staring in shock from her back door.

Well, she had been staring in shock from her back door. Now she was turning and running into her house for her life.

Unfortunately, Melissa's sidecar was right behind. It roared into the house after her. Mrs. Tubbs threw a look over her shoulder and let out a scream as they raced past her antique Louis XIV dining set . . . her Italian marble fireplace . . . her baby grand piano—all the way to her front entry hall.

In a flash of inspiration, Mrs. Tubbs reached for the front door, threw it open, and leaped aside . . . just as the sidecar zoomed past, bounced down the porch steps, and out onto the street.

It was a close call, but Mrs. Tubbs' clear thinking had saved the day. She took a deep breath and smiled in triumph . . . until she turned back into her living room and saw the muddy tire tracks running the entire length of her new white carpeting.

Then there was the other matter. The one of her having to leap aside again as Sean, desperate to save his sister, roared through her living room on his motorcycle.

"S-s-o-o-r-r-r-y-y, Mrs-s-s. Tub-b-b-b-s-s-s," he shouted as he bounced down her front steps and out into the street.

Mrs. Tubbs wanted very much to shout back an angry insult, but it's hard to shout out angry insults when you're busy passing out from shock.

WEDNESDAY, 06:54 PDST

Not far away, KC, Spalding, and Bear quickly closed in on the stranger. He was just ahead. Any second now and they would have him.

They came upon an intersection. The stranger faked to the right, then turned hard to the left. For a moment he'd outmaneuvered them.

But not for long. The kids slid their bikes into a sharp turn and continued the chase.

"You're not getting away this time!" Spalding shouted.

"Yeah, that's right!" Bear shouted. "You're . . . you're not getting away this time." (Bear's originality was about as good as Herbie's coordination.)

Once again the three of them closed in.

They came upon another intersection. This time the stranger turned hard to the right.

A good move . . . except that Sean and Melissa were coming around that very same corner from the opposite direction. The stranger veered to the left and just managed to slip past them.

His pursuers were not so lucky.

"AUGH!" Melissa cried.

"AUGH!" Sean cried.

"AUGH! AUGH! AUGH!" KC, Spalding, and Bear cried.

It was beautiful, all five kids shouting in perfect five-part harmony. But before they had time to start up a singing group or record a CD, they smashed into one another in the world's second biggest pileup.

(The first was back on page 26.)

It was just like old times as all five began untangling their arms, legs, and other various body parts.

But as much as Sean wanted to stick around and brag about whose concussion was the biggest, he knew he had to catch the stranger. He had to get to him before he reached his creepy house. Sean staggered to his feet and headed for the motorcycle. The fall had shut down the engine, and he was going to climb back on and restart it.

"I'm going after him!" he shouted to Melissa.

"Not without me, you don't," she yelled as she clambered to her feet and hobbled toward him. It's not that she was being brave, she just figured nothing else could be as frightening as what she'd already been through. (Of course she was dead wrong, but at the moment there was nobody as smart as you or me hanging around to tell her.)

Sean righted the motorcycle, and Melissa hopped on the seat behind him. He kicked the starter and it fired up. After revving the engine and leaving the required patch of rubber on the pavement, the two were once again headed down the street. Slobs faithfully followed, barking and baying all the way.

Back at the accident, Bear knew every inch of his body was either bent, stapled, or mutilated. But at the moment, there was something of even greater concern. "Ah, man," he whined. "My belt buckle's scratched. They scratched my belt buckle!"

But KC had other things on her mind. "Come on," she ordered. She rose painfully to her feet and began disconnecting the various parts of her body from the various parts of their bikes. "It ain't over yet."

Meanwhile, the stranger raced toward his spooky old house at the end of the block. He hopped the curb and continued up his sidewalk toward the porch. As he approached, he reached down and pulled another lever on his bike. Suddenly the front door flew open and the porch stairs flattened out, turning the steps into a smooth ramp. In a flash he shot up the ramp and disappeared into the house.

A moment later Sean and Melissa reached his yard and hopped off the motorcycle.

"Come on," Sean yelled. "Let's hurry!"

Seeing the forbidding old house and the scary darkness inside, Melissa suddenly had second thoughts.

"Come on," Sean cried, "we gotta follow him inside!"

Melissa sighed. "I was afraid you were going to say that."

Together with Slobs, they raced up the ramp, across the porch, and squeezed through the door . . . just before it closed, sealing tightly shut behind them.

At least they were inside, safe and sound.

Well, at least the inside part was right. Because they were anything but safe. . . .

8

Creepy Creepings

The door had shut behind Melissa, Sean, and Slobs with an ominous *thud*.

Inside, the house was darker than a piece of black licorice stuck inside the finger hole of a black bowling ball, stuck inside a dark bowling bag, stuck inside an even darker closet . . . at midnight.

In other words, the place was dark.

"Sean," Melissa whispered. "Sean!"

"Present," he answered.

"I can't see a thing."

"Me neither. Wait a minute."

A moment later Sean's tiny penlight came on. "We

may not have all the fancy electro gizmos," he said, "but at least we've got this."

The tiny beam darted about the room, revealing nothing but cobwebs covered in dust. The walls weren't much better. They hadn't seen a paintbrush in years. And what furniture the two saw was draped in old sheets. In short, the place was creepy in a major Freddy Krueger sort of way.

"Uh . . . Sean?" Melissa whimpered. "Maybe it would be a good idea for us to . . . uh, you know . . . *leave*?"

"Don't be such a chicken," he scoffed as he continued exploring with his light. "That jerk's got to be here somewhere."

"My point exactly."

"You're only afraid because you don't know," Sean answered. "Remember what Dad said about—"

"Excuse me," a voice interrupted.

Sean turned his flashlight on her face. "What?"

"It wasn't me," Melissa answered, shielding her eyes from the light.

Sean frowned. "You sure?"

"Of course I'm—"

"Excuse me," the voice repeated. "Excuse me."

Melissa's eyes darted about the room. The voice was

so close, but no one was there.

"Down here."

She glanced at the ground. Still nothing.

"Here. Right here."

It was Slobs who finally spotted it. She gave a whine and nudged at Melissa's hand.

Sean was the next to see it. "Misty . . . it's your watch," he whispered. "It's . . . it's talking."

"No way," she scolded. "How could my watch possibly be—"

The words froze in her mouth as she glanced at her digital wristwatch. Inside it was the same electronic character they had seen on the computer . . . and on KC's game.

"Hi there," it said, giving them a wave.

Slobs whined again.

Sean was the first to find his voice. "Who . . . who are you?" he croaked.

"Let's cross that bridge when we burn it," the creature answered. "Right now, if you're still looking for that stranger, you might want to check out the stairs."

Melissa and Sean both turned to look up the stairway. For a moment Sean hesitated, then he quietly crossed to the steps and kneeled for a closer examination. Sure enough, there were fresh footprints in the dust.

"He's right," Sean said.

Melissa nodded and glanced down to her watch. But the little figure was already gone.

Melissa and Sean traded nervous looks.

Slobs whined.

"Well . . ." Sean took a deep breath. "I suppose we should take a look."

Melissa nodded. "I suppose."

But they both remained standing, neither moving. They weren't entirely sure why. The best they figured it probably had something to do with wanting to stay alive.

"So . . ." Sean said, "what are we waiting for?"

"Oh, I can think of a few hundred reasons."

"Come on, let's go." He turned and started toward the stairs.

Reluctantly, Melissa followed.

Sean took the first step. It groaned and creaked under his weight. "He'll never expect us to follow him up here."

"I can see why," Melissa answered as she carefully eyed the rickety stairs and railing.

"We'll have the element of surprise on our side," Sean whispered. "He'll never know we're here until it's too—"

Unfortunately, this was about the time when Sean's

foot tripped the laser beam motion detector. Suddenly there were more flashing lights than in an old disco movie. This, of course, was accompanied by the obligatory wailing siren and the prerecorded shouting voice:

"WARNING . . . YOU HAVE ENTERED
A RESTRICTED AREA.
TURN BACK AT ONCE.
WARNING . . . YOU HAVE ENTERED
A RESTRICTED AREA.
WARNING . . ."

So much for the "element of surprise."

Melissa turned to race back down the stairs until she felt Sean's hand reach out and grab her.

"Are you going to let a little alarm scare us off?" he shouted.

Melissa turned to him, eagerly nodding her head.

"Don't be such a coward!" he yelled.

She was about to ask him what sort of coward he wanted her to be when she saw movement behind him and up the stairs.

"It'll take more than a little alarm to stop us," he shouted.

With widening eyes, Melissa nodded even harder. "You're right," she yelled. "How 'bout a hundred beach balls!"

"What?" He turned to look up the stairs.

That's when they hit. Hundreds of beach balls, all bouncing and tumbling down on top of them, knocking them off their feet and very quickly and quite efficiently burying them over their heads.

WEDNESDAY, 07:14 PDST

Meanwhile, KC, Spalding, and Bear had pushed what was left of their broken bikes up to the stranger's house.

"There's the motorcycle!" KC shouted.

"Precisely," Spalding observed.

They dumped the bikes and started for the porch. But the closer they got, the more their courage faded.

"Go on up there and knock," KC ordered Spalding.

"Actually," Spalding coughed slightly, doing his best to cover his fear, "given the nature of the situation, I believe now is the appropriate time to allow ladies to go first."

"No way," KC shot back. "You're supposed to be the leader of this group."

"So?"

"So lead."

Spalding coughed again. "Actually, the sign of a good leader is one who delegates responsibility."

"Meaning. . . ?" KC demanded as she stepped up to him, clenching her fists.

Immediately Spalding changed course. He knew that this little girl was small, but he also knew she had a temper (and a pretty good right hook). "Meaning . . . uh . . ." His eyes landed on the third member of the group. "Meaning, Bear!"

"Huh?"

"Yes, I believe Bear here is much more qualified for the activity of banging on the door than either you or me. Wouldn't you agree?"

KC nodded, her temper already fading, as they both turned to Bear.

Back in the house, Sean, Melissa, and Slobs were busy climbing out from under the avalanche of beach balls.

"You okay?" Sean asked when he finally spotted Melissa's head bobbing among the colored balls.

She nodded, shoved a couple dozen aside, and finally struggled to stand. "Yeah, I guess."

Sean did likewise. He'd no sooner made it to his feet than he turned and started back up the stairs. "Come on."

"Sean . . ." she pleaded.

"Come on," he repeated. "What more can happen?"

Melissa groaned. "I'm sure we'll find out." With a heavy sigh thrown in for good measure, she turned and started back up the stairs with her brother.

As the newly elected door banger, Bear moved past KC and Spalding. He reached the top of the porch, crossed to the door, and executed his duties proudly . . . so proudly that the windows rattled . . . so proudly that the seismic station over at the college registered a 2.3 earthquake.

But there was no answer.

"Try it again," KC ordered.

Bear obeyed with the same pounding, the same rattling windows . . . and the same lack of results.

"What's all that banging?" Melissa asked as they continued up the steps.

Sean glanced back down at the closed front door. "I bet it's KC and the boys."

There was more pounding.

"Maybe we should let them in?" she offered.

Sean shook his head. "If we're going to crack this case, then we've got to do it on our own."

They continued up the stairs as quietly as possible, which really wasn't all that quiet considering each and every step had its own unique creak and grown. They passed several portraits on the wall beside them. Distinguished-looking folks . . . the type who looked like they'd just eaten lemons for breakfast and washed them down with a tall, cool glass of vinegar.

"Weird," Sean said as he leaned closer to examine one.

Slobs stretched toward them, giving one a sniff before letting out a little growl.

"They give me the creeps," Melissa whispered.

"What's the big deal?" Sean asked. "They're just paintings."

As if on cue, all of the portraits suddenly slid down, revealing very large catapult arms behind each and every one.

Melissa gasped. Not so much at the sliding portraits or even at the catapult arms. It was the banana cream pies loaded in each one of those arms that caught her attention.

The very same pies that suddenly flew from the catapults directly at them.

"Duck!" she shouted.

But she was too late. Pie after pie came flying, hitting their faces, their bodies, their arms and legs. And just when every part of their bodies was covered with banana cream . . . the catapult arms loaded up, and a whole new round of pies came flying.

Outside, Bear had finally worn himself out knocking on the door. It was about this time that Spalding had another plan. A brilliant plan. A genius plan. A plan that made it clear why he was the leader of the group.

"Hey," he said, "why don't we go around and knock on the back door?"

By the time the pie attack had finished, it looked like an entire bakery had exploded . . . all over Sean, Melissa, and Slobs. Covered in smashed bananas, pie crusts, and whipped cream, they wiped out little holes for their eyes and sighed wearily. Then slowly, resentfully, they continued their climb, trudging up the stairs, dripping pie parts everywhere they stepped. It was a humiliating experience, and neither said a word . . . although, Melissa thought, there was more than the usual amount of slurpings, lickings, and burpings coming from both Slobs' and Sean's direction.

At last they reached the top of the stairs. Battered by beach balls and pelted by pies, they were definitely not having one of their better days. But at least they had arrived. Now all they had to do was check out the rooms in the hall. The stranger had to be hiding in one of them.

Sean reached for the first door. "Well," he said, taking a deep breath, "here goes nothing."

Unfortunately, he couldn't have been more wrong. For as he pulled open the door, a panel in the ceiling over their heads slid open. Hearing the sound, all three tilted back their heads to see . . .

Two dozen ketchup bottles. All poised and ready to fire.

"Oh no," Melissa groaned.

"I'm afraid so," Sean sighed.

The bottles opened fire, gushing thick red streams of goo all over them. Sean coughed and spit; Melissa screamed and choked; Slobs howled and slurped and drank.

And still the attack continued.

The thick, slippery goo made it almost impossible to see, let alone stand. And before they knew it, all three were slipping and sliding.

Trying to keep his balance, Sean stumbled back against the stair railing. Unfortunately, it was as old as the rest of the house, and it did little to support him. He immediately broke through and started to fall.

"Sean!" Melissa yelled.

He grabbed hold of the small portion of railing that stuck out. He kicked and struggled, trying to get a better grip, but everything was coated in slick ketchup. His feet dangled a good thirty feet over the entry hall below, and each kick caused more of the railing to give way.

"Hang on!" Melissa shouted as she did her best to slip and slide toward him. "Hang on!" But the railing creaked as more and more of it tore loose.

Sean looked over his shoulder and saw the floor below. *Far* below. He scrambled harder, causing more of the railing to give way.

"Help me!" he shouted. "Misty!"

"Hang on!" She continued fighting to get to him. But between all the slipping and sliding, she made little progress.

"Help me!"

"I'm coming, Sean, I'm com—"

Suddenly the last of the railing broke lose, and Sean started to fall.

"AUGHHH—"

But before he could complete the cry, another pair of hands reached out from the darkness. The gloved hands of the stranger grabbed Sean's wrists—and began pulling.

9

Secrets Revealed

WEDNESDAY, 07:35 PDST

Sean, Melissa, and Slobs found themselves standing in a huge attic with plenty of beat-up furniture, old storage trunks, and enough flickering shadows to give any horror movie the creeps.

But that was only the beginning. Because amidst all of these odds and ends sat the latest scientific equipment. Electronic this, computerized that . . . and of course the usual bubbling beakers, microscopes, and test tubes.

"Wow . . ." Sean said, taking it all in. "This place is incredible."

Melissa couldn't have agreed more.

"Why, thank you," the electronic voice answered. Melissa looked down at her watch, but he wasn't there.

"Over here," the little voice squeaked.

She turned to search the room.

"Over *here*."

At last she found him. He was on one of the computer screens. Sean had also spotted him and stepped in for a closer look. "Who exactly are you?" he demanded.

"Allow me to indoctrinate myself. My name is J.E.R.E.M.I.A.H."

"Who?" Melissa asked, moving in closer.

"Actually my full name is the *Johnson Electronic Reductive Entity Memory Inductive Assembly Housing*."

Sean nodded, pretending to understand. "Oh, right, of course."

Melissa gave her brother another one of those looks.

"But my friends call me Jeremiah. Well, actually, uh, I don't have any friends, but if I did have friends, that's what they'd call me 'cause that's what Doc, there, calls me."

Sean and Melissa turned around to see the mysterious stranger standing at one of the computer terminals. His back was to them as he pulled out the circuit board from his black overcoat. The very same circuit board he had stolen from the station.

"Hey," Sean shouted, "that's my dad's!"

But the stranger didn't respond. Instead, he began to carefully install it into one of the large control panels beneath a computer monitor.

Sean started toward him. "Hey! Listen, mister, I'm talking to you."

There was still no reply. So he grabbed the stranger's arm and turned him around. "I said that's my—"

But Sean came to a stop when he finally saw that the mysterious man wasn't a man at all. It was a woman. A pretty woman at that. No more than twenty-five years old.

Melissa gasped in surprise.

Sean stuttered, "You're not a he . . . you're a . . . a *she*."

Without a word she spun around and returned to her work.

"And not a very friendly she," Melissa added.

"You have to understand." It was Jeremiah again. Only now he was on another computer monitor, much closer. "Doc is one of those super-intelligent genius types."

Sean nodded. "I almost got straight A's once . . . well, in one subject . . . well, if you call recess a subject." He turned to the Doc for a response, but she didn't even acknowledge that he'd spoken.

"She's also deaf," Jeremiah explained. "Can't hear a thing."

"Oh."

Melissa stepped forward. "That doesn't give her the right to go around stealing stuff."

"Stealing?" Jeremiah asked. "I'm afraid you're barking up the wrong flagpole. We don't steal."

"What do you call taking those circuit boards?" Melissa asked.

"We didn't take them, we bought them. We paid for every one."

"Yeah, right," Sean scoffed.

"Sure we did. We left the money right there in the tea kettle."

"That was you?" Melissa asked.

"You ain't just a-whistling through your hat."

Meanwhile, KC, Spalding, and Bear were in the back alley, busy climbing over the wrought-iron fence. Well, KC and Spalding were busy climbing over the fence. Bear, because of his awesome weight, was having a little trouble getting off the ground.

After his fifth or sixth fall, he finally growled, "I quit. Let the Hunter kids handle it."

"And have them get all the glory for runnin' the creep out of town?" KC asked. "No way. He's ours, not theirs. Now come on."

"But . . ." Spalding cleared his throat. "Have you seriously considered our options once we all arrive?"

"What?"

"Once we climb over this fence, how exactly do we make our entrance?"

"See that greenhouse over there?" KC pointed to a large glass-enclosed building attached to the side of the house. "We'll bust out some of them glass windows and sneak in. Now get your rear over this fence, Bear, before I climb back over and kick you up it."

Back in the attic, Melissa continued asking Jeremiah questions. "I'm still not exactly sure who or what you are."

"I told you, I'm a *Johnson Electronic Reductive Entity Memory*—"

"I know, I know," Melissa interrupted. "But what does that mean in English?"

"You're an artificial intelligence?" Sean ventured.

"Exactly," Jeremiah nodded his little head up and down. "I was invented by the Doc here."

Sean continued. "And since you're electronic, you can somehow appear on LCDs, TVs, or computer screens?"

"Right again."

"But why did you bring us here?" Melissa asked.

Sean turned to her. "What do you mean? He didn't bring us here."

"Sure he did. He was the one who woke us up in the station so we'd see Doc. He was the one who made sure we followed her. He was also the one who told us she was up the stairs." Melissa turned back to the computer screen. "In fact, everything you did was to make sure we discovered you two, wasn't it?"

Jeremiah gave a sheepish grin. Then suddenly he disappeared.

"Hey, where'd he go?" she asked.

"Over here."

They turned to see the little guy on a monitor directly

above Doc. But the woman paid no attention to him. She was so involved in her work that she ignored everyone.

"You're right," Jeremiah admitted. "I did bring you here."

"But why?" Melissa asked.

"The way I figure it, we need each other."

Sean moved closer. "What do you mean?"

"As you may have noticed, the Doc and I, we don't have the best social graces."

"You mean like her being rude and ignoring us?" Melissa asked.

"Or not knowing the difference between buying and stealing?" Sean added.

"Or having everyone want to run you out of town?" Melissa continued.

"Or—"

"Well, yeah . . ." Jeremiah coughed nervously. "If you want to get specific. Anyway, I figured you could help us get along with people in the real world, and we could help you with all the electronic gizmos and gadgets your agency needs."

"How'd you know we needed that stuff?" Sean asked.

"Like you said, I get around."

"So you want to form a partnership?" Melissa asked.

"More like a corporation," Jeremiah answered.

"Hmmm . . ." Sean began to think—something that always made his sister a little uneasy—"Bloodhounds, *Incorporated*."

Jeremiah nodded. "You hit the nail right on the foot."

But before Misty could raise any questions or at least suggest they think it over, they were interrupted by a loud hum. They looked over to see Doc turning all sorts of knobs and switches.

"What's she doing?" Melissa shouted as the noise grew louder.

"Trying to increase soybean productivity in the greenhouse through accelerated electromagnetic radiation."

"Oh, right," Sean nodded, once again pretending to have the slightest clue of what Jeremiah was saying. "I thought it was something like that."

But you could barely hear him over the increasing noise.

"Come on down," KC called up to Bear, who was

now clinging to the top of the fence for his life. "It's not that far of a drop."

Bear looked down and gave a shudder. Maybe it wasn't a long drop by KC's standards, but with Bear's weight, he figured he'd hit the ground and keep going until he stopped somewhere in China.

Besides there was the other problem. The one involving his belt loop. The one that was hung up on the fence's long, pointy spike.

"Just let go," KC said.

"But—"

"We haven't all day," Spalding insisted.

"B-but . . ."

"Come on!"

It was obvious his partners were getting a little impatient. So against his better judgment and at the risk of ruining his size seventy-five Dockers, Bear let go.

Unfortunately, the fence didn't . . . at least not of his Dockers.

RIIIPPPPPP!

He hit the ground with a groan (and far less pants than when he started out). Together the three of them headed for the greenhouse.

"Hold it!" Spalding whispered. "Wait a moment."

113

"Now what?" KC sighed.

"Observe the size of those greenhouse windows."

"So?"

"So they are far too small for any of us to crawl through . . . even you, KC."

"So what are we supposed to do?" she said.

Spalding glanced around the yard until he spotted some distant garbage cans. "Are you still in possession of your lighter?" he asked.

"Always," she said, pulling it from her jeans.

"Then I suggest we grab some paper, break out a pane of glass, and proceed to smoke him out."

Back in the attic, the hum increased.

Slobs began to howl.

Sean and Melissa traded nervous looks.

Come to think of it, Jeremiah didn't look quite so relaxed, either.

The beakers on the lab bench began to shake. Then the lab bench holding the beakers began to shake. Then the floor that held the lab bench that held the beakers began to . . . well, you probably get the idea.

"Wh-wh-wh-a-t-t-s hap-p-p-p-en-ing-ing?" Sean shouted.

"I-I-I'm not s-s-sure," Jeremiah yelled. "I-I-I think sh-sh-ee m-m-might have the p-p-power up a little h-h-high."

There was a sudden, blinding flash of light. Then everything went dark . . . except for a faint green glow that started to grow brighter and brighter.

"Uh-oh," Jeremiah's little voice sighed. "I hate it when this happens. . . ."

10

Wrapping Up

WEDNESDAY, 07:52 PDST

Out in Doc's backyard, KC, Spalding, and Bear arrived at the garbage cans. They were just pulling out some dried newspaper and preparing to light it when they were interrupted by a tremendous . . .

KUH-TWHACK.

KC's head jerked up. "What was that?"

"I'm not sure," Spalding answered, looking around. Then with a trembling voice, he continued. "However, I fear it might somehow be associated with the greenhouse over there."

KC and Bear turned to the greenhouse. It looked just like it had before. Plenty of plants on the inside, plenty of glass on the outside. There was only one minor difference. . . .

The entire greenhouse was filled with a pulsating, blue-green glow!

"What's going on?" KC demanded.

Before anyone could answer, the lighter in her hand began to glow the same color. Then suddenly, without notice, it was pulled from her grip and shot across the yard until it hit the side of the greenhouse. But instead of falling to the ground, it simply stuck there against the glass. Apparently, the entire greenhouse had accidentally become a giant magnet.

"Oh no," Spalding said. But he wasn't referring to the lighter. He was referring to his fancy Rolex watch, which had also begun to glow. He stared in astonishment as it slowly rose into the air (dragging his wrist and arm with it). Then like the lighter, it, too, began heading toward the greenhouse (not only dragging Spalding's wrist and arm, but his entire body).

"Somebody help me!" he shouted, doing his best to dig in and stop the movement. "Help me!"

"Take it off!" KC shouted. "Take off your watch!"

"It cost $350!" he cried. "You're craz—" But that was all he managed to get out before he lost his footing and shot across the yard . . . wrist first.

He joined the lighter sticking to the side of the greenhouse.

"Uh-oh," Bear groaned. He was looking down at his giant Texas belt buckle. Like the greenhouse, the lighter, and the wristwatch, the buckle had also started to glow. He looked up at KC, gave a weak sort of smile, and then suddenly was whisked across the lawn to the greenhouse, where he hit the glass and remained stuck to its side.

Fortunately for KC, she wasn't wearing any weird pieces of metal. She thought she was perfectly safe . . . until she felt a tingling in her mouth and noticed the blue-green glow coming from the braces on her teeth. She barely had time to scream before she was dragged across the lawn with lightning-like speed.

Now all three kids were smooched up against the greenhouse glass, unable to free themselves . . . unable to move.

Back in the lab, there were more sparks and smoke than a Fourth-of-July celebration gone haywire. Melissa,

Sean, even Slobs dove and scrambled under nearby tables and counters for cover.

And then just when it looked like everything was about to go into major meltdown, it all stopped. The loud hum slowly wound down, the sparks quit, and the smoke began to clear. A moment later the lights flickered and finally came back on.

Doc looked over at Jeremiah. Jeremiah looked over at Doc.

"Oh well." Jeremiah shrugged. "I guess it's back to the ironing board."

Outside, the greenhouse also went dark. Suddenly all three kids slipped from the window and dropped to the ground. But they didn't stay there. Immediately, they were back on their feet, racing toward the back gate for all they were worth.

"Get me out of here!" KC cried. "Get me out! Get me out!"

Spalding and Bear would have answered, but they were too busy doing their own screaming and running to save their own lives.

Back in the lab, things quickly settled down to normal. Well, except for the occasional sparking and the puffs of smoke that still drifted by.

"So," Jeremiah cleared his throat. He was in the monitor above Doc again. "What do you two say?"

"About what?" Sean asked as he crawled out from under the table.

Melissa joined him. "About forming a corporation?" she asked.

Jeremiah nodded. He motioned toward Doc, who was staring at the smoldering circuit board and scratching her head, trying to figure out what went wrong. "Believe it or not, she's one of the best inventors in the country. You two could really use her help in coming up with all your spy gizmos and gadgets. And we could sure use your help in learning how to fit into the community."

Sean and Melissa exchanged glances.

"What do you think?" Sean asked.

Melissa scrunched up her eyebrows and thought. "We should probably check with Dad. I mean we hardly know these two."

121

"You know he'll say yes."

"Probably."

"And of course he'll use it as a chance to say I told you so."

"What do you mean?" Melissa asked.

"By finding out who Doc was and what really happened at the station, we finally overcame our fear, didn't we?"

Melissa nodded slowly.

"So what do you say?" Jeremiah's crackly little voice called from the monitor.

Sean turned to him. "I say we give it a try."

Melissa grinned. "Me too."

"Okie-dorkie!" Jeremiah cried.

Catching on to the excitement, Slobs also began to wag his tail and whine.

"A partnership," Sean exclaimed. "Just the four of us."

Slobs' whines turned to howls.

"Oh, sorry, girl—make that five."

"Bloodhounds, Incorporated," Melissa shouted as she raised her hand and gave her brother a high five. Doc had seen their movement, but when they turned to her, expecting her to join in, she simply looked at them, then returned to her work.

"Over here," Jeremiah motioned for them to approach his screen. "Over here!"

With arms still raised, Melissa and Sean crossed to the monitor, and little Jeremiah threw his hand against the glass, joining them in a three-way slap. It was a pact, an agreement.

"Bloodhounds, Incorporated," Jeremiah squeaked. "I like the sound of that."

Apparently, so did Slobs, who started barking as Jeremiah repeated the phrase one last time.

"Bloodhounds, Incorporated!"

Sneak Preview

The Mystery of the
Invisible Knight

THURSDAY, 21:30 PDST

The alley was dark.

Real dark.

Not dark like the garage when you can't find the light and wonder if the shadow over there is the rake or really a monster waiting to eat you. And not dark like your grandma's cellar when she asks you to go down and get a can of peas. (Thanks, Grandma, I just love risking my life for a green vegetable.) No, I mean dark like being a blind man in a shadow-filled room looking for a black cat that isn't there. That kind of dark. In other words . . .

It was kinda hard to see.

That's exactly what Mr. Morrisey was thinking as he stepped out of his jewelry shop and into the back alley.

125

Once again the streetlight had burned out, which meant he had to fumble with his keys to lock the back door. But that was okay because he'd soon be home eating a delicious plate of overcooked cauliflower and broccoli while watching a *Gilligan's Island* rerun. He'd then top off this incredibly exciting evening by soaking his dentures. (Does this guy know how to have fun or what?)

But tonight . . . tonight would be just a little different because—

Clank.

The loud, metallic sound echoed through the alley. Mr. Morrisey's heart skipped a beat.

Clank. Clank.

Mr. Morrisey's heart skipped two beats.

The sound was closer . . . and quickly approaching. The old man thought of running. But at his age, he'd be lucky to outrun a dead turtle. And the best he could make out, this was no turtle.

"Who . . . who's there?" he called.

Clank.

"I said, who's—"

126

Clank. Clank.

Now Mr. Morrisey could finally make out a shape. A very large shape. He began to back away.

Clank! Clank! Clank!

Slowly, it emerged into a faint pool of light. Now Morrisey could see it clearly. It was a knight! From the days of King Arthur. And even in the dimness, its suit of armor seemed to glow.

Mr. Morrisey continued backing away as the knight continued closing in, its metal armor crashing with every step.

Clank! Clank! Clank!

Suddenly the thing came to a stop.

The old jeweler stood watching, shaking like a plate of Jell-O on a jackhammer, as the knight slowly raised its arm. Then even more slowly, it lifted the face visor of its helmet to reveal . . .

Nothing!

That's right, it was completely empty—as in the visor was open, but nobody was home!

Mr. Morrisey could take no more. He fainted. Just

like that. Out cold. Not dead, but not waking up for a while, either.

Then the knight calmly closed its helmet and turned back toward the open door of the jewelry store.